OH ME, OH WHO AM I?

by Dr. Taneshia Knight Shelton

Oh Me, Oh My, Who Am I?
Copyright ©2015 by Taneshia Knight Shelton
Illustrations ©2015 by Amariah Rauscher

All rights reserved. This book or any portion thereof may not be reproduced or used in any manner whatsoever without the express written permission of the publisher except for the use of brief quotations in a book review.

Printed in the United States of America by TKS Productions
www.taneshiaknightshelton.com

ISBN-13: 978-0692402153
ISBN-10: 0692402152

Library of Congress Control Number: 2015912172

The text of this book is set in 24pt DKClochard font.
The illustrations in this book were created using watercolor and charcoal.

To every little girl with an ounce of doubt—you CAN conquer the world!

Once upon a time, there was a little girl. She would sit in her room and stare at the mirror. Every night she would wish for her Fairy God-Mother to appear to help her answer this one question she could not make disappear.

One day, the little girl got her wish! With the blink of an eye her Fairy God-Mother appeared. Her Fairy God-Mother asked, "Little girl, Little girl, what question do you have?"

The little girl answered, "Fairy God-Mother, I feel so down. I feel like I have lost my crown. So, I need your help to help me see all that I am meant to be. There is just one question that needs a reply. Oh Me, Oh My, Who am I?"

The Fairy God-Mother beamed with glee as she was ready to tell the little girl just who and what she was destined to be.

Little Girl, Little Girl,

You are a daughter of the King!

Little Girl, Little Girl,
You can do and be anything!

Little Girl, Little Girl,

You are blessed and highly favored!

Little girl, Little girl,
You are strong and empowered!

Little Girl, Little Girl,

You are beautiful and bold!

Little Girl, Little Girl,
You are courageous and free!

Little Girl, Little Girl,
You are confident and unique!

Little Girl, Little Girl,
You are love and laughter!

Little Girl, Little Girl,
You are powerful and divine!

 Little Girl, Little Girl,
   You are smart and ambitious!

Little Girl, Little Girl,

You are healthy and healed!

Little Girl, Little Girl,
You are a leader and not a follower!

Little Girl, Little Girl,
You are a princess becoming a queen!

Little Girl, Little Girl,

You are an amazing sight to see!

Little Girl, Little Girl,

You are an unforgettable masterpiece!

Little Girl, Little Girl,
You are a priceless possession that can't be bought!

Now, go conquer the world with all you have been taught!

About the Author

Taneshia Shelton lives in Georgia with her husband and two sons. She holds a Ph.D in Public Health from Walden University. "Oh Me, Oh My, Who Am I?" is her debut children's book. You can find out more about Taneshia by visiting her on the web at:

www.taneshiaknightshelton.com

You can follow Taneshia on her Instagram @iamdrtks or like her Facebook Fan Page at:

www.facebook.com/taneshiaknightsheltonphd

Made in the USA
Middletown, DE
04 September 2015